ANIMALS AT RISK

To everyone who has worked
in any way to save whales.
J.A. T.H.

The author and publisher wish to thank
Martin Jenkins for his invaluable
assistance in the preparation of this book.

First published 1992 by Walker Books Ltd
87 Vauxhall Walk, London SE11 5HJ

This edition published 1998

2   4   6   8   10   9   7   5   3   1

Text © 1992 Judy Allen
Illustrations © 1992 Tudor Humphries

This book has been typeset in Times New Roman.

Printed in Hong Kong

British Library Cataloguing in Publication Data
A catalogue record for this book is available from the British Library.

ISBN 0-7445-6228-7

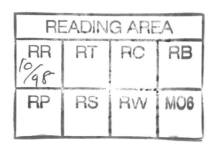

WHALE

Written by
Judy Allen

Illustrated by
Tudor Humphries

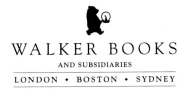

WALKER BOOKS

AND SUBSIDIARIES

LONDON • BOSTON • SYDNEY

"I've never seen the moon so big or so brilliant," said
Anya's mother, as she kept the wheel of the little cabin
cruiser steady. "It's a magic night, now the storm is over."

"Good magic or bad magic?" said Anya, doubtfully.
She thought the moon looked fine, but she wasn't so
happy about the lightning which was still chasing itself
to and fro in the distance, just where the sky became
the sea and the sea became the sky.

It usually took three hours to cross the water between the island, where Anya's grandmother had her house, and the mainland, where Anya and her parents lived. Always before they had travelled in daylight, but this time they had had to wait for the sudden, fierce storm to move on its way, and they were late.

The sea looked much deeper at night than it did in the daytime, and it also looked wider, and stronger, and stranger. It was not rough, there were no waves hitting against the bow of the boat, but there was something that Anya's father called "a heavy swell". This meant that the sea made big, slow movements underneath the boat, as if it were breathing long, slow breaths – or as if something enormous were moving just below its surface.

While Anya's mother steered the boat towards their home harbour, whose lights looked as tiny and distant as stars, her father tried to make the radio work properly. The storm had left the air full of electricity and the words were coming out of it mixed up with sparkling noises, as though a thousand needles were being shaken in a glass box.

Anya thought she would rather listen to the clattering and scratching of the needles than to what the radio was saying. It was talking – on and on and on – about an oil tanker, which had run aground in the bad weather, and about rescue operations and a vast oil slick.

"Are people drowning?" said Anya, holding tightly to the edge of the boat and looking at the deep, dark water.

"No," said her father. "Everyone's safe."

"The people are safe," said her mother, "but just imagine what damage that oil slick will do."

Anya knew what her mother meant. A flood of oil would come out of the side of the wrecked tanker and spread over the surface of the water. It would choke the fish to death, it would stick to the wings and beaks of the sea-birds so

they couldn't fly or feed. It might even catch light and send flames running across the surface of the sea, threatening anything that was on it.

"Are we near it?" she asked nervously.

"No," said her mother. "It's a long way away."

"Oil slicks travel," said her father, gloomily.

"Depending on the wind and the tides, it could come our way in a day or so."

The moon and Anya stared at the swelling sea.

"I know why people used to believe in sea monsters," said Anya. "It does look as though something huge is making the water bulge up and down. Especially back there."

"It's the current," said her father, with his eyes on the radio.

"It's the pull of the moon," said her mother, with her eyes on the distant light of the harbour buoy.

"It *is* a sea monster," said Anya, suddenly frightened, her eyes on something far behind – but not far enough behind. "Something rose up just now and went down again, and it wasn't water."

"Where?" said her father.

"There!" said Anya.

"I can't see anything," said her father.

"It's not there now," said Anya in a small voice. "It may be coming closer – underneath."

"Don't panic," said her mother. "What did it look like?"

"Big and dark and wet," said Anya.

"Like the sea?" said her father gently.

"It wasn't the sea, it was different."

Anya's mother slowed the boat and let it drift a little sideways, so that she could look behind them.

"Oh, there," said Anya and her father together, as a dark mass rose up through the surface of the moonlit water for a second and then sank out of view.

"Whale!" whispered Anya's mother. "It's a whale, it really is."

Anya's mother kept the engine turning gently, so that the boat stayed more or less in one place, and they got out the binoculars and took it in turns to stare at the sight that the moon was lighting up for them.

"It's a humpback whale," said Anya's father, "but it doesn't look right. It's floating and sinking, it's not swimming and diving."

"I think it's in trouble," said Anya's mother, when she had the binoculars. "I wonder if it's injured in some way."

"There's something with it," said Anya, when it was her turn.

"There's something – it's hard to see – oh – it's a small one, it's a very small one, it has a baby."

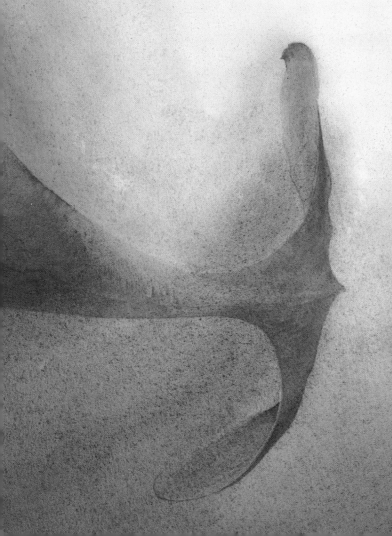

"I know what's happened," said Anya's mother, sounding as if she wished she didn't. "The tanker broke up in the breeding grounds. She's just had her calf and she's had to out-swim the oil slick. She's exhausted."

"But she *will* be all right?" said Anya.

No one answered her.

"*Will* she be all right?" said Anya, wondering if she wanted to hear the answer.

"I think she may not be," said her father, quietly, as the shiny curve of the whale's back slid down under the water again. The baby went down with her. "She hasn't the strength to keep herself and her calf at the surface. Whales breathe air, Anya, like us. I think she may be drowning." He turned back to the radio.

"But can't we do something?" said Anya, horrified.

Her mother put her arms around her. "There's nothing we can do," she said, and her voice sounded as if she might cry. "She is very big and very heavy – there is no way we could support her while she rests. I think we'd better go on home."

"We can't *leave* her," said Anya, staring and staring at the place where the whale had disappeared.

"We can't help her," said her mother, "and I don't want to watch her die."

"I'm trying to get the coastguard on the radio," said her father, "just in case anyone else can do anything. But I can't get through."

The whale's back appeared again, but she did not rise as far out of the water as she had before. She was gone again, almost at once.

"She's not blowing," said Anya's mother, sadly. "She's not breathing."

"I can't *bear* it," said Anya, and her voice began to get louder, "please help her, someone must save her, *do* something, *please*."

The moon watched the dark swelling water.

Strange sounds began to fill the air, coming from everywhere and nowhere – trumpeting sounds, almost like elephants, but not elephants, and then strong steady chirping sounds, rather like birds, but not birds.

"What's that?" said Anya's mother.

The sounds grew stronger. They shivered through the sky as though the moonlight had a voice. They echoed deep under the water and made the boat shudder.

"Look," said Anya. "Oh look!"

Far behind them, and way over to each side of them, the water was moving. Great, dim shapes were breaking the surface, gleaming silver in the moonlight. Breathy waterspouts were rising in glittering columns into the air.

Massive tails were flicking upwards and then sinking in slow, deep dives.

"Whales are coming!" said Anya's mother. "It must be the rest of the herd."

Enormous though they were, they were powerful
and streamlined and they surged through the water
at astonishing speed.

"We should get into shore," said Anya's father,
dreamily, "they could sink us." But he didn't move.

"Yes," said Anya's mother, but she didn't move either.

Anya said nothing – she just stared and stared as the
nearest whales submerged and then rose again, slowly,
steadily, lifting the mother and her calf between them.

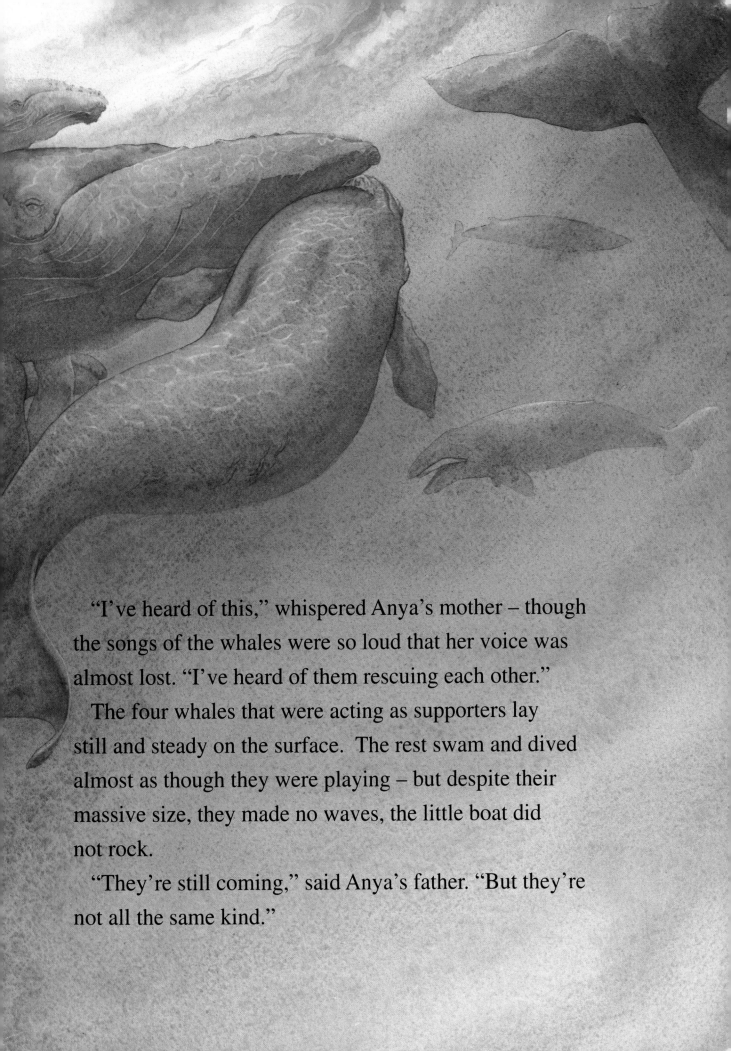

"I've heard of this," whispered Anya's mother – though the songs of the whales were so loud that her voice was almost lost. "I've heard of them rescuing each other."

The four whales that were acting as supporters lay still and steady on the surface. The rest swam and dived almost as though they were playing – but despite their massive size, they made no waves, the little boat did not rock.

"They're still coming," said Anya's father. "But they're not all the same kind."

The moonlight showed humpback whales, with long flippers and tiny back fins, the smooth backs of great right whales, the huge, blunt head of a sperm whale, and, in the distance, a basking blue whale, so vast that it looked like a small island. There was even a narwhal, with a single corkscrew tusk, like a sea unicorn.

"I don't understand," said Anya's mother.

Something else was odd, too. As the whales moved
in the water, the moonlight showed great, dark gashes in
their sides. Some of them even had harpoons buried deep
in their bodies, the shafts sticking out at odd angles. Every
one of the whales that surrounded the female and her calf
was badly injured – but not one of them seemed to mind,
not one of them seemed affected by its wounds.

"This is the strangest sight anyone ever saw," said
Anya's mother.

"This is magic," said Anya.

Afterwards, none of them could say how many whales they saw that night, and none of them could say how long it was before the female humpback recovered – but they all agreed on one thing. In the very second that she began to move on, in the very second that she no longer needed help – every single one of the other whales vanished. They didn't swim away, they didn't submerge, they just weren't there any more, and where their songs had been, there was silence.

When they reached land, Anya and her parents asked everyone they knew, and a lot of people they didn't know, if they had seen what had happened. No one had.

"We're the only ones," said Anya's mother, "who know that the spirits of the dead whales came to help her."

Later, there was a report on local radio – a female humpback whale and her calf had been sighted, swimming strongly towards the south, well away from the spreading oil slick:

"We're not quite the only ones who know," said Anya. "The whale and her baby – they know, too."

WHALE FACT SHEET

THERE ARE MANY DIFFERENT sorts of whale, including the 30-metre-long blue whale, the largest animal that has ever lived. Whales are found in seas and oceans all over the world, but are now most numerous in the cold waters of the Antarctic. All the different whales have been greatly reduced in number, and some, such as the blue whale and the northern right whale, are now very rare and may become extinct. Others, like the sperm whale, and the humpback whale in the story, are still fairly common, and have a good chance of survival if they continue to be protected.

◆ WHAT ARE THE DANGERS FOR WHALES? ◆

Whales have been hunted by people for many thousands of years, for their meat, oil and bones. Despite this, most kinds of whale remained quite common until recently. In the twentieth century, however, whales have been killed in enormous numbers by factory whaling ships, and several species are now threatened with extinction.

◆ IS ANYONE HELPING WHALES? ◆

Yes. In 1986, under pressure from conservation organizations like WWF (World Wide Fund for Nature) and Greenpeace, the International Whaling Commission stopped all large-scale whaling. People in areas such as Greenland and Alaska are still allowed to catch a few whales, as they have done for many centuries.

◆ ARE EFFORTS TO SAVE WHALES SUCCEEDING? ◆

The ban on commercial whaling has allowed most sorts of whale to start increasing in number, but it may have come too late for some. A few countries would like to start commercial whaling again. If this is properly controlled, it should not endanger any whale species, but many people are worried that this may not happen.

◆ IS THERE ANYTHING YOU CAN DO? ◆

Yes. You can join the junior section of WWF or Greenpeace, or persuade your family or your school to join.

WWF
Panda House
Weyside Park
Godalming
GU7 1XR
United Kingdom

Greenpeace
Canonbury Villas
London
N1 2PN
United Kingdom

◆ ABOUT THE AUTHOR ◆

Judy Allen worked as a book editor before
becoming a writer in 1973. Since then she has
written many books for children and adults,
including the award-winning children's novel,
Awaiting Developments, as well as compiling
Walker Books' *Anthology for the Earth*.
Judy Allen lives in London.

     Judy says the hopeful note at the ending of
Whale was inspired by the fact that "in real life
whales do come to each other's rescue".

◆ ABOUT THE ILLUSTRATOR ◆

Tudor Humphries lives in Devon with his wife and
three children. He has worked as a landscape
painter, a children's book illustrator and a life-
drawing teacher. He is also a qualified costume
and set designer, and this theatrical training has
had a profound effect on his ideas about drama,
lighting and atmosphere in pictures.

     Tudor says that he overcame the problems
he had painting tropical night waters by spending
time diving and taking photographs underwater,
while travelling in Greece.